# Flanimals

by
## Ricky Gervais

Illustrated by
## Rob Steen

ff

With many thanks to Lee

First published in 2004
by Faber and Faber Limited
3 Queen Square London WC1N 3AU

Printed in Belgium by Proost

A CIP record for this book
is available from the British Library

ISBN 0–571–22077–0

10  9

# Contents

**There are a few things you need to know about Flanimals. And when you do, I'd keep them to yourself if I were you.**

# Chapter 1

## Spotter's Guide

# Coddleflop
## *(Ovarian Fliphanger)*

Slurdles around absorbing stains and puddles.
Its only defence is to flip over to protect its soft top.
Unfortunately, its bottom is equally soft and is
instantly squashed if trodden on.

# Plamglotis
## (Taslo Epiglug)

Born without feet, it swallows its hands to walk
on to find food. Obviously, when it finds food
it can't eat it because its mouth is full.

# Mernimbler

### *(Gruntling Flumpamorphis)*

Mernimblers live on honey water and
the softer bits of clouds. They stay this way for some time,
then turn into adults when someone says "Oh, look
at those cute Mernimblers, I think I'll stroke one."

# Adult Mernimbler

## (Gruntling Flumpamorphis)

Eats everything it sees
and dies of chronic indigestion.

# Grundit

### (Grundoidian Yobjammer)

Staggers around half-witted and grumpy,
trying to start trouble. Its favourite hobby is using
the Puddloflaj as a form of transport, but it always
falls off, causing the bumps on its head. Luckily the
brain is too small to be affected.

# Puddloflaj
## *(Blobbulous Boinglubber)*

Cowardly wobbler that spends its days avoiding the Grundit.
The Puddloflaj looks like a useless fat blob. It actually doesn't
have an ounce of fat on it – it's water retention. In fact it's nearly
100% water, sort of like filling a balloon from a tap.
Baby Puddloflaj can be used as water bombs.

# Flemping Bunt-himmler

## *(Guzzle Sprout Flemper)*

**Feeds on baby Mernimblers and replaces them in the nest. He is exposed when they all turn into adults and eat him.**

# Underblenge

## *(Ekino Plunge-Dermer)*

Snerbulent splench-sucker that captures prey
by sticking to their faces and suffocating them – its
suckers are impossible to prize off. Unfortunately,
it can't catch anything as it can't move from
the rock it was born on.

# Splunge
## *(Jello Snurbloid)*

Quite literally a bag of nerves.
So utterly terrified of everything it splunges at birth.
This causes both parents to do the same.

# Honk
### *(Hagen Splurg-Klanger)*

Moley squit that sleeps all day, until
for no reason it makes the loudest noise on the planet,
causing its nose to trumpet up to fifty times normal size.
It then falls to the floor exhausted and fast asleep.

# Hemel Sprot
## (Podis Reversis)

Rushes across the guddle deserts on its
wobble pod, only looking where it's been, never
where it's going. Eventually dies by bumping
into the Sprot Guzzlor.

# Sprot Guzzlor

## *(Guzzlank Plod)*

**Gruntloid in build but related to the Anker.
Eats Hemel Sprots but is terrified of adult Mernimblers.**

# Clunge Ambler
## *(Humpulous Lug)*

This sweaty little waddle-gimp shuffles around trying to cuddle things. He is weird and smells, so is constantly being beaten up and buried. He never learns his lesson and always tries to find and cuddle the Flanimal that buried him. The Flanimal usually buries him again.

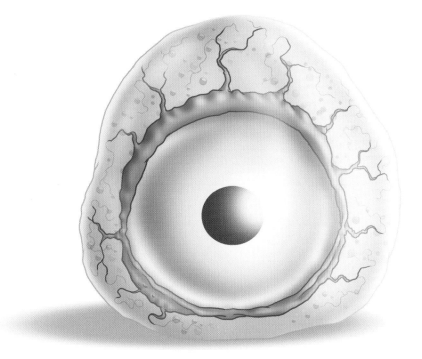

# Wobboid Mump
### *(Lumpus Chuck-Goggler)*

One of the most useless organisms in the universe.
It is basically an eye in jelly. It spends most of its time
looking around trying to find reason in its existence.
It never finds it as it is blind.

# Sprine Bloat-Trunker

## *(Puddly Groid Bulb)*

**Sprouts up explosively from a fungal spume puddle
outside the sewage  pump of the Sprog and Hemel Sprot
recycling plant. It immediately joins the queue
to be recycled.**

# Print

## *(Addle-Sprungnurdler)*

Small sprooding creature that
dives around, sometimes off tall rocks,
but always manages to land on its head.
They usually die from landing badly in
strong wind and spraining their ankle.

# Gum Spudlet

## *(Dentoid Mashler)*

**Grundit food.
It's not happy about this but it can't bite back.**

# Sprog
## *(Scousious Angroid)*

Honionoidly angry about its breath, the Sprog
bounces and squeaks around until it is chewed
up and spat out by a Grundit.

# Munge Fuddler
## *(Flange Snatchling)*

Despite being too mungey for its own
good, it persists in fuddling everything it sees.
Eventually gets battered when it fuddles
the wrong thing.

# Frappled Humpdumbler
## (Omloid Valve-Winkler)

This squiddy monj-dingler scrundles along
snuffling in one direction and oggling in the other.
Sounds weird, doesn't it? It isn't.

# Offledermis

## *(Gibletous Oderis)*

Born completely inside out.
Lives inside itself to avoid its
own smell.

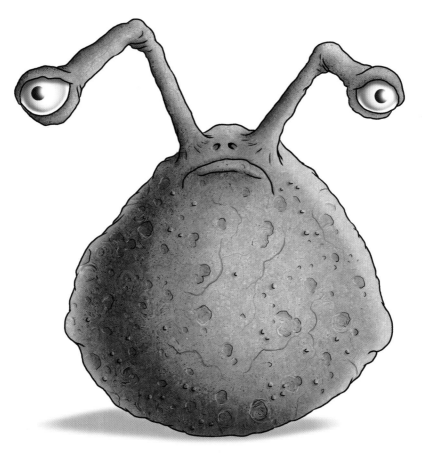

# Plumboid Doppler

## *(Scrotus Boggelum)*

This lumpy squint-sack is both
wormily turgid and yet slumpily flembal
at the same time. Apart from this
it is totally normal.

# Chapter 2

# Flanimal Behaviour

**Flemping Bunt-himmler in Mernimblers' nest**

**Baby Mernimbler halfway through transformation**

The world record for the quickest a Flemping Bunt-himmler
has been ripped to bits by Mernimblers is 12 seconds.
As it climbed into the nest it foolishly commented on
how cute the Mernimblers were.

The adult and baby Mernimbler weigh the same.
This makes the baby Mernimbler the densest
Flanimal on the planet.

**Grundit kicking a Gum Spudlet**

## Grundit about to ride Puddloflaj

The Puddloflaj hates being ridden by the Grundit,
that's why the Grundit does it. If the Grundit jumping on the
Puddloflaj is too big for it, the pressure can pop the
Puddloflaj's eyes out. The furthest a pair has popped
out is 19 feet. The Puddloflaj couldn't pick them
up as it couldn't see them.

## Herd of Blunging

Blunging are social creatures
and live in herds. When fully
grown they are the fastest of the
Flanimals, so fear no predator.
Baby Blunging are not so fast,
and taste brilliant.

**Clunge Ambler being attacked by gang of Sprogs**

No reason for this, they're just vicious.

# Newborn Plamglotis

Everyone finds newborn babies messy disgusting little creatures, apart from the mother that is. This is not the case with a newborn Plamglotis – its mother finds it disgusting too.

**Munty Flumple staring at a Puddloflaj**

**The Puddloflaj looks worried.**
**The Puddloflaj always looks worried.**

## Baby Munty Flumple

A baby Munty Flumple is the cutest thing in the universe.
Don't you just want to squeeze its head and bite its face?
The adult Mernimbler does.

**Grundit stamping on a Coddleflop**

This is one of the Grundit's favourite pastimes.
Looks cruel, doesn't it?
The thing is, it's nothing personal, it just likes the
sound they make as they squelch then pop.

**Sleeping Honk**

# Splunge splunging

As you know, being born causes splunging in both baby and mother. Some Splunges have foolishly tried to avoid this by never becoming pregnant. This never works because they have already exploded when they were born.

The world record for a simultaneous mass splunge is 37. Twelve mother Splunges gave birth at the same time with the fathers present. That's 24 adults and 13 babies (there was one set of twins).

## Munge Fuddler about
## to fuddle an Underblenge

**As you know, this is a pointless exercise,
as the Munge Fuddler's best fuddling takes place
on the mungier, dangly bits that hang from a
Flanimal's underparts. It can't get to the Underblenge's
underparts, so 'a-fuddlin' it is a waste of time.**

# Sprog and Hemel Sprot
# Recycling Plant

**Grundit dipping a Gum Spudlet into a Coddleflop**

Looks cruel, doesn't it?
Actually it improves the flavour.

# Chapter 3

# Flanimal Testing

# Which Flanimal would make the following footprints?

13. If a Puddloflaj's eyes pop out, why can't it pick them up?

14. What adds flavour to a Gum Spudlet?

15. Which Flanimal sproods the most?

16. What is the Glonk's favourite pastime?

17. The Plamglotis only eats two things in its entire life. What are they?

18. Which way is the Hemel Sprot running?

**Left**

**Right**

Incidentally, the Hemel Sprot isn't a true Sprot at all, it's actually part of the Ployb family. You can see why it's called a Sprot though, can't you? Looks just like one, doesn't it? And anyway, they couldn't call it a Hemel Ployb, as there's no such thing.

**19. Which Flanimal's babies make the best water bombs?**

**20. The Underblenge is both hungry and cold come winter. Why doesn't it migrate to a warmer climate?**

**21. What Flanimal is this?**

# Answers

1. Adult Mernimbler
2. Sprot Guzzlor
3. Underblenge
4. Blimble Sprent
5. Clunge Ambler
6. Glonk
7. Honk
8. Plamglotis
9. Print
10. Sprog
11. Sprine Bloat-Trunker
12. Hemel Sprot

13. Because it can't see them.
14. Coddleflop brain juice.
15. The Print.
16. Doing absolutely nothing.
17. Its hands.
18. Right.
19. Puddloflaj. It's the Grundit that uses them as water bombs because it likes chucking stuff around. It also uses Coddleflops as frisbees. The bad news is, it can only throw each Coddleflop once as this kills them. The good news is, there are so many Coddleflops around the Grundit never runs out.
20. It can't move from the rock it was born on because of its powerful suckers.
21. Clunge Ambler.

# Flanimal Scale Chart

**Human**

**Adult Mernimbler**

**Blimble Sprent**

**Blunging**

**Clunge Ambler**

**Coddleflop**

**Flemping
Bunt-himmler**

**Frappled
Humpdumbler**

**Glonk**

**Grundit**

**Gum
Spudlet**

**Hemel Sprot**

**Honk**

**Baby
Mernimbler**

**Munge
Fuddler**

**Munty
Flumple**

**Offledermis**

**Plamglotis**

**Plumboid
Doppler**

**Print**

**Puddloflaj**

**Splunge**

**Sprine
Bloat-Trunker**

**Sprog**

**Sprot Guzzlor**

**Underblenge**

**Wobboid
Mump**

## Other Flanimals

I'd love to tell you about the Bletchling,
the Gernloid and the Weezy Tong Nambler,
but this book ends here...